Out of Sight

Jan Pritchett
Illustrated by Trish Hill

Rigby

In the Ground

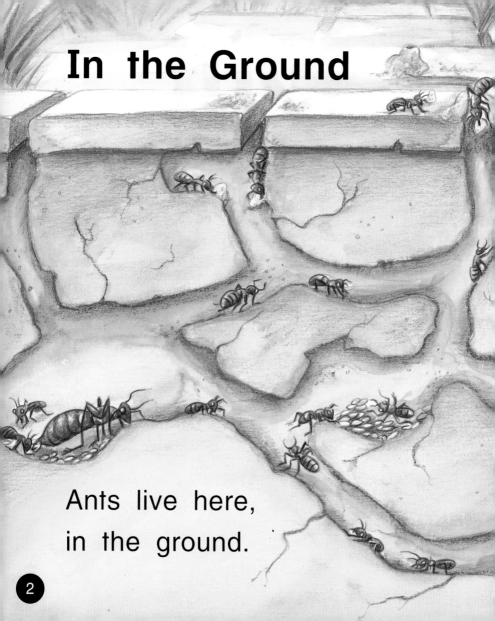

Ants live here,
in the ground.

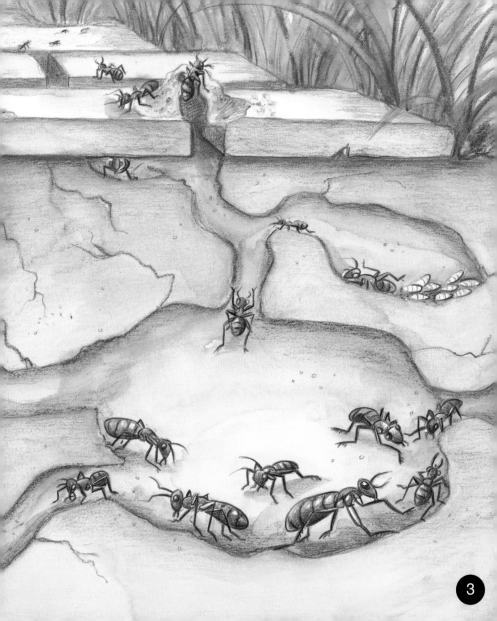

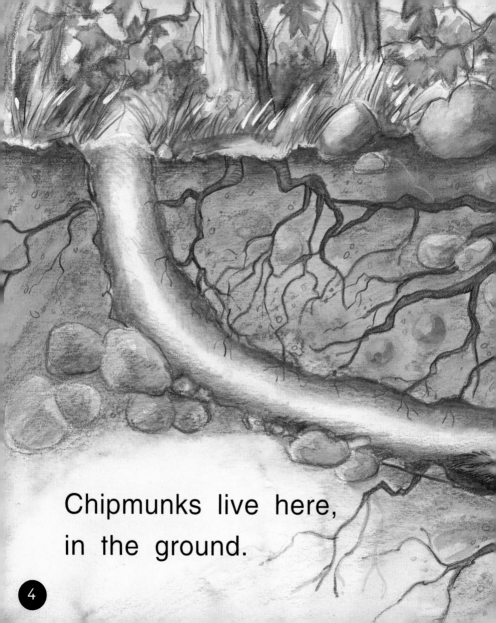

Chipmunks live here,
in the ground.

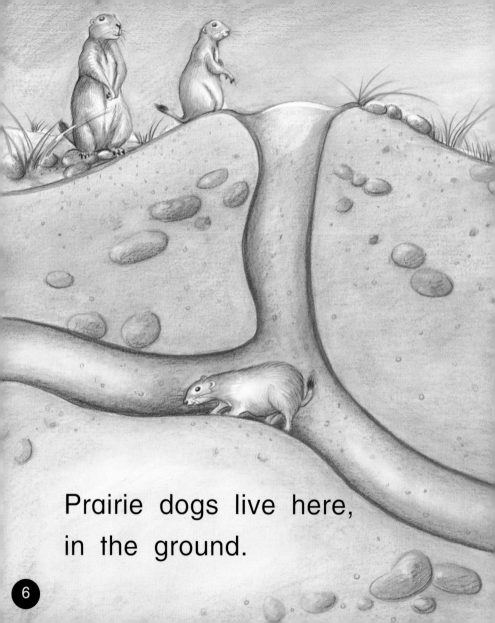

Prairie dogs live here,
in the ground.

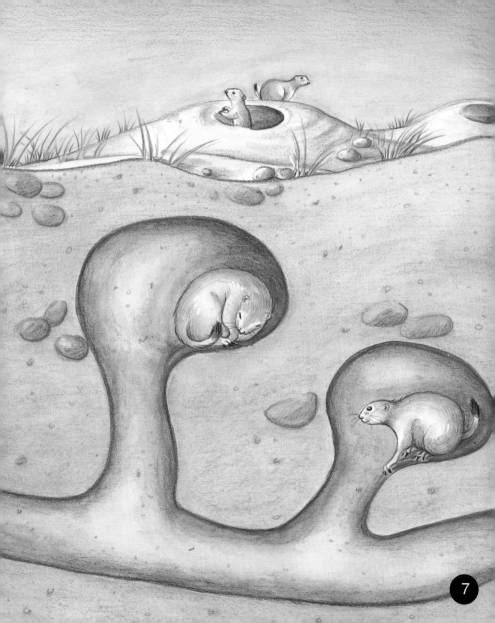

In the River

Beavers live here,
in the river.

Otters live here,
in the river.

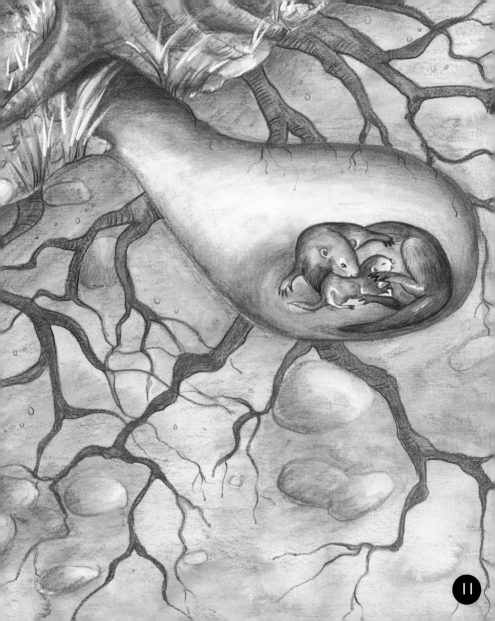

In the Trees

Bees live here,
in the trees.

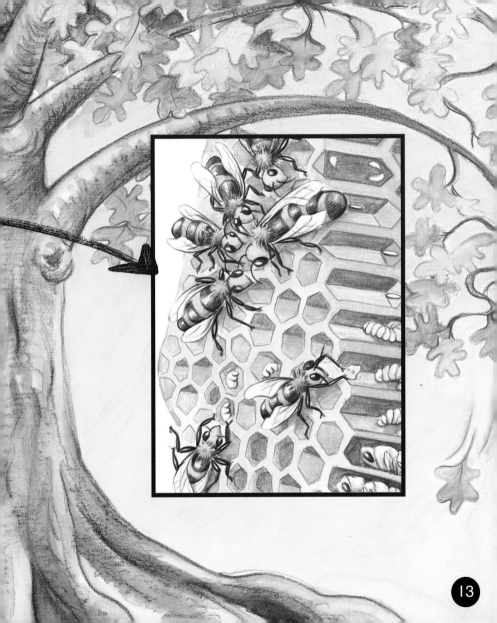

Woodpeckers live here,
in the trees.

Index